Kids love
Choose Your O...

"Choose is so addicting! I read EVERY
ending, just to see what happens!"
Scott Graham, age 12

"I think it's way more exciting when you
choose your own fate instead of just reading
a book the normal way. *Choose Your Own
Adventure* lets you be the main character!"
Megan Meany, age 10

"I love all the different endings.
Your choices decide the outcome."
Karianne Morehouse, age 12

"I love these books! I like to choose which
way to go and then go back if I make
a bad decision."
Jessa Sargent, age 11

Watch for these titles coming up in the
Choose Your Own Adventure® series.

Ask your bookseller for books you have missed
or visit us at cyoa.com to learn more.

INCA GOLD

BY JIM BECKET

ILLUSTRATED BY SUZANNE NUGENT
COVER ILLUSTRATED BY JOSE LUIS MARRON

CHOOSE YOUR OWN ADVENTURE® CLASSICS
A DIVISION OF

CHOOSECO
WAITSFIELD, VERMONT

Illustrated by: Suzanne Nugent
Cover illustrated by: Jose Luis Marron
Book design: Stacey Boyd, Big Eyedea Visual Design

For information regarding permission, write to:

CHOOSECO
P.O. Box 46
Waitsfield, Vermont 05673
www.cyoa.com

ISBN-10 1-933390-20-4
ISBN-13 978-1-933390-20-8

Published simultaneously in the United States and Canada

Printed in the United States of America

0 9 8 7 6 5 4 3 2 1

To Lydia with love

BEWARE and WARNING!

This book is different from other books.

You and YOU ALONE are in charge of what happens in this story.

There are dangers, choices, adventures, and consequences. YOU must use all of your numerous talents and much of your enormous intelligence. The wrong decision could end in disaster—even death. But, don't despair. At anytime, YOU can go back and make another choice, alter the path of your story, and change its result.

You and your best friend Sally discover some strange straight lines in the middle of the Peruvian jungle. Could it be the mythical Lost City of Gold from ancient Incan tales? You persuade Sally to spend your grant money on a trip to Peru to find out. But you must tread your way into the depths of the jungle carefully. There are many seekers after the ancient treasure. And more than a few of them would rather not have any competition . . .

It's past midnight, and you're struggling to stay awake in front of the computer screen. For as long as you can remember, you've been fascinated by ancient civilizations. A few years ago, using a home computer, you deciphered the ancient Egyptian tablet "Rondus X." As a result, you were awarded the prestigious Youth Archeologist Research Grant. You and your friend Sally, whose father is an engineer for NASA, have been working for months on a special computer program. Your program is designed to analyze highly detailed NASA satellite photos of the earth's surface in order to detect evidence of ancient ruins hidden beneath desert sands or jungle foliage.

While you're interested in all ancient civilizations, Sally is particularly interested in the Incas of Peru. She went to grade school in Peru, where her father worked at a satellite tracking station. There, she became fascinated by these ancient people who worshipped the sun. The Incas considered gold to be the "sweat of the sun" and silver the "tears of the moon." And at one time they ruled an area of South America larger than Texas.

You've programmed the high-speed computer with all known Incan building styles and settlement patterns. Now the computer whirs as it scans photos of remote jungles of Peru, areas of the ancient empire of the Incas.

Turn to the next page.

The computer suddenly beeps. A straight line appears on the screen. Your program is based on finding straight lines, because straight lines indicate that people have altered nature.

"Hey, all right!" you shout, and Sally rushes to pull the corresponding NASA photo from the files.

You can't see any lines on the photo, nor indications of any Inca-style buildings. Sally scans the photo with a magnifying glass. "There is something. Look here."

You look at the photo again, then glance back at the computer. Could this line of dots on a computer screen point the way to the fabled ancient Inca Lost City of Gold? That's where the

Incas hid the priceless royal treasury after being defeated by their Spanish conquerors more than four hundred and seventy years ago.

"It's probably the remains of a farmer's cattle pen or a rare rock formation," Sally says as she studies a large map and locates the place near where two rivers join in an isolated valley.

"No! Look how extensive it is. It has to be the ruins of a city. Maybe even the Lost City of Gold," you exclaim.

"I'm afraid those stories of a city of gold are just old legends," Sally says.

"The only way to find out is to go there," you point out.

"You're joking, right?" Sally counters.

"No. We have the grant money, what better way to use it?" you reply.

"No, I mean that's the Soledad region. It's called the 'Green Hell' for good reason. Hundreds of explorers have died in there. The few who survived came out crazy." Sally shudders at the thought.

Turn to the next page.

"But we know just where we have to go. It could be the greatest archaeological discovery of the century," you exclaim.

"That wouldn't be all that hard considering we're only a few years into the new century," Sally teases. Sally likes to be very precise. Sometimes it can be a little annoying especially when you want her to be as excited as you are.

"Come on, Sally! You know what I mean. It's got to be the treasure hunt of a lifetime!" You're distracted from your enthusiasm by a passing shadow. Someone is outside the glass door of the computer room.

"Hey!" you call toward the door. The shadow moves. You run out just in time to see a man darting down the hall.

Sally reaches your side. "I bet it's the same person who broke into our filing cabinet last week!"

You know your program is the envy of other treasure seekers, especially those who see it as a way to get rich quick.

"If he was listening, he knows we've discovered a lead in Peru," you say. "But he doesn't know where. I'm tired of looking at a computer screen. Let's prove our program really works. Let's go to Peru. And let's hope we're not followed!"

Turn to the next page.

6

You and Sally look out the window of your plane as it makes its final approach to the airport in Cuzco, Peru. The sun glimmers off the roofs of the city, which was once the capital of the Inca empire. Toward the east, the snow-capped mountains of the Andes rise over twenty thousand feet.

Sally is flipping through a book about the Spanish conquistador Francisco Pizarro. "It's incredible how many people Pizarro killed because he was so greedy for gold. It says here," she says as she points to a paragraph in the book, "that when Pizarro came to Peru in 1532, he invited the Inca emperor, Atahualpa, to a banquet. The Incas came unarmed. Pizarro had his soldiers slaughter all the emperor's men and took Atahualpa prisoner."

You've read other history books that tell this same story, but you listen to Sally anyway. You remind yourself that you're not motivated by greed. After all, you wouldn't keep the gold. It will all go to a museum—if you find it, that is.

Go on to the next page.

Sally continues reading, "Atahualpa offered to buy his freedom by filling the large room he was in with gold—."

"But Pizarro strangled Atahualpa before the gold arrived," you interrupt, "and the porters who were bringing the priceless royal treasure to the Spanish hid the gold they were carrying."

"It was never found." Sally looks at you expectantly.

"Until we came along, that is," you say optimistically. "If our computer program is on target, we'll find the Lost City of Gold."

Turn to the next page.

8

As your plane taxis toward the terminal, you see an all-black jet. A golden puma with emerald eyes is painted on the nose of the jet. You recognize the symbol—it's the mark of the ancient Incas.

"Whose plane is that?" you ask the passing flight attendant.

"Paul Leduc's," she answers as she hurries by.

You've heard of the eccentric billionaire recluse. Paul Leduc is obsessed with collecting the world's greatest art treasures—treasures he allows no one else to view. And now, as you watch Leduc's plane, you see a familiar-looking man descending the plane's steps.

"Isn't that Professor Maloder?" you say, pointing the man out to Sally.

"It could be—it looks like him," Sally agrees. "But I thought he was still in jail for smuggling art objects out of Egypt."

Sally's expression changes suddenly. "Do you think it was Maloder who broke into our files?" she asks. "Maybe that's why he's with Leduc. They've come to steal the gold!"

Turn to page 10.

Sally visits you in the Cuzco hospital, where your badly broken leg is in traction. She's grateful to you for saving her life, but neither of you feels like celebrating. No one on the train survived the crash.

Sally shows you a newspaper photo of the Cuzco railway station after the train hit the concrete wall at nearly ninety miles an hour. Fortunately the station had been cleared of people a few seconds before the train hit.

"Well," you tell Sally, "even if I could walk, I don't think I have any desire for treasure hunting now."

"As soon as you get your walking cast"—Sally manages a smile—"we'll walk straight to the plane to go home."

The End

"Wait a minute, Sally," you say calmly. "Let's not jump to conclusions." Which is a switch as you're the one who usually jumps to conclusions. You have to admit that it's some coincidence they're here the same day you arrive.

You watch as two suspicious-looking men, one very tall, the other with a shaved head, follow Maloder out of the plane. They seem to be looking directly at your plane!

As your cab pulls away from the airport, you notice that Maloder's henchmen are directly behind you in a dark blue car. Another coincidence?

After checking into a hotel, you and Sally discuss what should be your next step. You could set off right away for Soledad to try to find the place indicated on your computer screen. But what if Maloder is following you? Maybe it would be better to play tourist for a few days?

If you decide to head for Soledad right away, turn to page 12.

If you go to Machu Picchu as tourists, turn to page 17.

Before setting out for Soledad, Sally calls Maria, an old school friend. Maria should know the best way to travel to the region without being followed. She invites you to come right over to her house.

From a window in the hotel lobby, you can see across the small square to a sidewalk cafe. Sitting at a table are the two men who followed you from the airport!

"Sally, I've got an idea!" you whisper. "Let me take a taxi in the opposite direction of Maria's house. That'll get them off your trail so you can get there safely. We'll meet back here."

"All right," Sally agrees. "But be careful. What do we do with our map and the satellite photo?"

You hurry back to your room, and after considering a number of hiding places, you finally slip the map and photo behind the bathroom mirror.

You hail a cab and as it pulls away from the hotel, you look back at the cafe. Maloder's men are no longer at the table.

Driving past the cathedral in the *Plaza de Armas*, you see the dark blue car behind you.

Go on to the next page.

"Driver, turn here!" you order. You point to a narrow side street that climbs up one of the steep hills above Cuzco. The dark blue car follows, comes up fast from behind, and rams the cab! Your startled driver curses, speeds up, and tries to outrun the pursuing blue car in the narrow crowded streets.

Near the top of the hill, the driver stops the cab, opens the door, and roughly pushes you out *"Es su problema, señor,"* he yells. He drives away leaving you alone on the dirt street just as the dark blue car squeals around a corner and heads right at you!

Turn to the next page.

You run up a set of steps carved out of the hill, steps that lead to a maze of shacks. There's no way a car can follow you. The only way for it to get up the hill is along a narrow, twisting road that would take forever. Your heart pounds. You gasp for breath in the thin air of high-altitude Cuzco. Then you see him!

Maloder's tall man is coming after you. Leaping over a fence into a yard, you knock down a sheet from a clothesline. Apologizing to the woman shouting at you, you hurry past. She pins the sheet back up just as the tall man knocks her down. They both fall, tangled in the sheet.

Turn to the next page.

16

You arrive at flat ground, rousting a bunch of chickens that squawk in every direction. A thousand feet below you stretches the city of Cuzco. You're standing at the edge of what appears to be a cliff. It's an incredibly steep slope of stones and gravel. To attempt to descend it is almost certain death. If you could stay on your feet and brake yourself going down, like a skier, you might survive. But if you fell, you'd roll faster and faster till you crashed on the jagged rocks below.

Outside a shack you see a beat-up old car. It has no doors, but the four tires look okay. Maybe it will start. You might have a chance to escape down the narrow road.

The tall man runs into view. You can see the twisted smile on his face as he spots you. He knows he's got you now.

If you decide to jump in the car,
turn to page 42.

If you decide to risk the cliff, turn to page 21.

The next morning, you and Sally, wearing sunglasses and carrying cameras, step out of the hotel looking like perfect tourists. The satellite photo and map are safely in your backpack. Across the street you spot one of Maloder's henchmen sipping coffee at a cafe table.

He doesn't move as your cab drives away.

Cuzco's old railway station is noisy and crowded with tourists and locals hawking souvenirs. You and Sally manage to find seats on the modern diesel train headed for Machu Picchu. A big tourist attraction, Machu Picchu is an Inca fortress on top of a mountain crag. It was never found by European explorers. An American named Hiram Bingham discovered it in 1911.

The train snakes its way through the spectacular Urubamba gorge. The tracks follow the river on one side. On the other side, the mountains thrust sharply up to pierce the morning clouds.

"When we discover the Lost City of Gold, they'll build a railway like this for tourists," you tell Sally.

"I'm just glad we're not being followed and can enjoy the trip," Sally answers, leaning comfortably back in her seat.

Turn to page 19.

Two hours later you're in a bus climbing up a dirt road cut into a steep mountain. Below you is the railway station, and almost straight up above you is Machu Picchu.

Soon you're standing in the midst of the stone ruins of Machu Picchu. It's like being on the roof of the world. You marvel at the work of the Inca masons, huge carved stones perfectly fitted together. Terraces, built to grow food for the inhabitants of this last Inca bastion, drop down the back side.

Sally points to the sky. "Look! A hang glider."

Sure enough, a lone figure hanging beneath a red triangular wing leaps off a peak above the ruins and swoops down toward the valley.

"Some Japanese are making a television commercial," notes a passing tour guide.

"Come on. Let's hike the trail that leads up to where the hang glider jumped," you suggest. "Another trainload of tourists has just arrived." You push past the crowd and start up the trail.

Finding a quiet place, you sit down to catch your breath. The view is spectacular. You look down the trail and see less than 100 yards back Professor Maloder and his two henchmen.

"Sally! Come on! Quick!" you whisper. You rush up the trail away from the ruins. The faster you go, the faster the three men follow. There's no doubt they're after you!

Turn to the next page.

The trail steepens as it winds around the peak. You lose sight of your pursuers when the trail bends. Ahead of you on a ledge are three hang gliders, leaning against the rock face. Should you and Sally take a glider trip off the side of the mountain to avoid Maloder and his men?

You hear the sound of rhythmic voices. Looking across to another mountain, you see a very strange group of people sitting in a circle. At one point in the trail, the two mountains are so close you think you could almost jump across. In fact, if you could get across, you could hide yourself within the group. But if you were short on the jump, you could fall two thousand feet below.

You can hear your pursuers approaching. If you keep going up the trail, you'll be trapped at the summit. You have to do something, and quick.

If you want to risk flying a hang glider, turn to page 23.

If you want to risk leaping to the other mountain, turn to page 36.

You hesitate at the edge of the cliff, trying to build your courage. The pounding footsteps of your pursuer get closer.

You step off, planting your feet in the gravel, bending your knees and leaning forward. With your feet acting as brakes, you shift your weight as if you're skiing, and zigzag down, setting off an avalanche of stones behind you.

You lose your balance for a second, fall back, but quickly right yourself before being buried by the tumbling stones in your wake.

The slope starts to level out, and you break into a run across the flat terrain, chased by a shower of stones. You did it! The soles of your feet are burning, but you're alive. You look back up. The tall man stands at the edge of the cliff. An angry scowl has replaced his smile. You know he won't risk following you down.

Walking quickly through a backyard, you come to a city street. As you make your way to a bus stop, you hear from up on the hill the screech of a speeding car taking the sharp curves. You look up just in time to see the dark blue car skid out on a turn and tumble off the cliff. Even at a distance you can hear the crunching sounds as it rolls, bounces, and crashes.

An ancient bus chugs up to the stop. You hop on, knowing that, at least now, you won't be followed. But after what nearly happened, you're worried about Sally. You wish the old bus would go faster. You're anxious to get back to the hotel.

Turn the next page.

Sally greets you excitedly in the hotel lobby and starts to talk before you can tell her about your narrow escape.

"You won't believe this but my friend Maria is now a pilot," she says, "and she has her own plane! We could parachute right into Soledad and save ourselves weeks of hiking."

I know you've parachuted in the desert," you say. "But isn't it pretty dangerous to jump right into the jungle?"

"The map shows an open space about ten miles from our target," Sally replies as she follows you up the stairs to your room.

"But there are two rivers almost as close," you explain. You're thinking it might be safer traveling on the ground.

"I asked about that," Sally says. "We could drive over the Andes, then take one of the rivers, but river travel is dangerous now. It's the rainy season."

Turn to page 34.

"I'll try anything once," you yell, grabbing a hang glider.

"Do just what I do!" Sally shouts as she snatches up one of the others and carries it over her head out onto the ledge.

You swing the bright yellow glider over your head. It's much lighter than you thought. Standing on the ledge looking down makes you dizzy. The station and the train look like toy models. Part of you is frightened, but part of you feels a strange urge to jump.

Sally buckles herself into a harness, then grasps the bar attached to the wing. Your shaky hands fumble with the buckle until it finally clicks into place.

Maloder charges into view just as two Japanese cameramen above you shout, "Stop! Stop! Thief!"

Sally leaps off, the tail of her hang glider just clearing the ledge.

You feel paralyzed. Maloder is coming full tilt at you.

Turn to the next page.

24

You step off the ledge into nothingness, just as Maloder lunges for you.

You're flying! The furious voices of men cursing you back on the ledge, some in English, some in Japanese, are quickly drowned out by the whistle of the wind in your ears.

Where's Sally? Did she crash? you wonder. Couldn't have. There! She's above you. She's skillfully caught an updraft. Now she swoops down alongside you.

"You've got the hang of it!" she shouts, giving you a thumbs up. She points down to the train and back toward the men on the ledge. The last train of the day is your only escape, and Maloder and his gang will be hurrying to get there before you.

Turn to the next page.

Sally swoops downward in a tight turn. As you push on the bar, the hang glider responds. You're getting the feel of it. If you weren't running—flying—for your life, your flight would be pure fun.

You look out to your left, right into the eye of an enormous bird. Its wingspan is as wide as your hang glider. A giant condor. A very rare sight. You go into a turn and the condor banks with you. Even though the bird looks fierce, with its hooked beak and bald neck, you're sure it's playing.

Approaching the valley floor, the condor flaps its wings to climb back toward the peaks, its natural home.

A crowd of tourists watches Sally gracefully land next to the station.

The ground is coming up at you much too fast. You push the bar forward as hard as you can so the tail of the wing will slow you. Here comes the ground! Boom! You hear something break, and end up in a heap.

"You okay?" Sally rushes to your side. You feel much better when you realize that what broke was a hang-glider strut, and not your leg.

Sally helps you out of the rig. "The train's leaving, hurry!"

As you settle into your seat on the speeding train, you see a jeep, churning up a cloud of dust, racing down the road toward the station. It will never catch the train you're riding. Maloder is too late.

Go on to the next page.

Sally and you are in the last car with a dozen tourists. You've had enough excitement for one day and doze off to the comforting clickety-clack of the rails.

You're roughly awakened when the train comes to a sudden halt, throwing you against the seat in front of you.

A moment later the door bursts open, and a fierce man in a camouflage uniform, waving a submachine gun, strides down the aisle. "Out! *Afuera!*" he screams.

Turn to the next page.

You, Sally, the engineers, conductors, and some twenty-five tourists line up along the tracks. Six guerrillas push and poke the passengers as they examine the tourists' passports.

The guerrilla who searches you is young, with classic Inca features. He goes through your backpack, sees the satellite photo but takes out your passport.

A helicopter thumps overhead. The heavyset leader of the band appears to order everyone back into the last car.

You stumble in the aisle, and the young guerrilla pushes you down on the floor, throwing your passport back and kicking you for good measure.

The conductor, lying next to you, whispers, "The guerrillas want to exchange some of their comrades in the city jail for us. The leader, *el comandante*, says they'll kill us unless the government frees their people."

Go on to the next page.

"Who are they?" you ask in a quiet voice.

"They dream of bringing back the old Inca empire, of making the Indians masters in their own house. They hate outsiders."

You wait on the floor for what seems an eternity. You know the guerrillas are negotiating outside, and that all your lives depend on the outcome.

El comandante enters the railroad car and shouts, "Stand up! We have made a deal. You will not be harmed. But we need one volunteer. We are leaving in an army helicopter, but we need one hostage with us to be sure the army will not shoot. We will all live if one of you steps forward."

He casts a cold eye on the hostages. The seconds tick away. You can see his anger is rising. He looks at two small Japanese girls who clutch their mother's leg. Might he choose these children—or Sally? Should you volunteer, taking the risk so everyone else will be safe? Or should you wait for your opportunity to do something to help the army capture these dangerous rebels?

If you decide to step forward to be the hostage, turn to page 43.

If you decide to play for time, turn to the next page.

You remain on the floor, barely breathing. No one steps forward. Most of the hostages stare at the floor as *el comandante* waits for an answer.

"Cowards!" he shouts. He looks directly at you. "Then we will have to choose someone."

"SEND THE HOSTAGES OUT FIRST!" booms a loudspeaker from outside.

El comandante rushes to the window, "No, we go first to the helicopter!"

Sweat pours down *el comandante*'s dark face as he turns to confront the hostages. He grabs Sally's arm. "This one is coming with us!"

"No! I'll go." You start to rise from the floor.

A rifle butt comes out of nowhere, knocking you down against the metal base of a seat. You lose consciousness.

Go on to the next page.

Shots from outside wake you. The railway car is empty. Struggling to your feet, you see people outside scatter to escape the bullets. Some of the hostages are free!

But others stumble back into the car—the two little Japanese girls and their mother, an English couple, and Sally. Behind them are the young Incan guerrilla and *el comandante*.

El comandante shouts an order to the young Incan guerrilla and rushes into the next car. Sally spots you, and the two of you duck down and move to the back of the car while the young Incan guerrilla has his attention on the others. The shooting stops outside.

Sally and you get through the door of the car onto the rear platform.

"Are you all right?" you ask urgently.

Sally nods, but you can see she's badly shaken.

The train starts with a jolt, throwing you both to the floor. Rapidly the train picks up speed, leaving behind the soldiers and the lucky hostages who escaped.

You stand up and see that, at this speed, it's too dangerous to jump off. The glass door behind you shatters. The young Incan guerrilla has a gun!

You and Sally duck, crawling a few feet to the side of the platform. A shot hits the door. The young Incan guerrilla is coming after you.

Turn to the next page.

You have nowhere to go but up. You help Sally onto the small ladder fixed to the rear of the railway car and climb quickly to the roof.

You move slothlike along the roof on all fours. The train, made up of an engine and cars, barrels along at top speed. In a curve you catch a glimpse of *el comandante* at the controls of the locomotive.

An army helicopter tries its best to keep up with the hurtling train. But threading through the narrow gorge is tougher than making the right moves in a high-speed video game.

Houses flash by in a blur as the train hits the outskirts of Cuzco. At this speed the railway station is only minutes away. And the station ends in a concrete wall! Is the guerrilla leader so desperate and enraged that he means to go into the station at eighty miles an hour?

Up ahead you see the bridge where the tracks cross the Urubamba River into the city. The river is narrow and deep at this point.

Turn to page 51.

Reaching in your pocket for your room key, you notice that the door is slightly ajar. "The maid must be cleaning up."

But when you open the door, you can't believe the sight before your eyes: clothes and papers have been strewn about, furniture overturned.

"I think an un-maid has been here," Sally jokes lamely.

You rush to the bathroom and reach behind the mirror. Your fingers touch the glossy surface of the satellite photo. Whoever ransacked your room didn't find the photo and map. Since it looks as if nothing in the room has been stolen, you're sure it was the papers that your mysterious intruder was after.

It's time to set out for Soledad. Should you parachute with Maria's help or travel by land and water?

If you decide to go by air and parachute in, turn to page 46.

If you decide to go by land and water, turn to page 55.

You back down the trail to get a good running start for your leap. "Let's go for it!" You shout to Sally, but more to encourage yourself. She can jump further than you can, so if you can make it, she will too.

You take off! Knees pumping high, feet flying over the packed dirt and stones of the trail, eyes fixed on the ledge. You hit the edge and leap out into space.

You land on the other side just at the edge, teeter back for a moment, then roll forward.

By the time you pick yourself up to encourage Sally, she's in the air. She lands at your feet, knocking you down. Laughing, you slap each other's hands like victorious athletes. From where you are now, what you just did looks impossible.

Some fifty people sit in the circle. They have to be the strangest tribe you've ever seen. Weird costumes, bright electric colors, and far-out hairdos. All are chanting, "Om Shanti, Om Shanti, Om Shanti . . ." A bearded man, dressed in white, seems to be their leader.

No one pays any attention to you as you join the circle. You borrow ponchos and cover yourselves, just as your pursuers appear on the other mountain. Maloder and his two henchmen look in every direction, including over at your group. Then Maloder leads his men on up the trail, confident he has you trapped at the summit.

Turn to the next page.

The bearded leader strikes a gong. The chanting rhythmically concludes.

An older woman with dyed red hair and enormous earrings smiles warmly at you. "Welcome. My name is Mariposa. Our leader's name is Baba Bubu."

Relieved to hear she speaks English, you ask, "What country do you all come from?"

"California," Mariposa whispers. We came here to chant for peace. Machu Picchu is a very special place, and tomorrow all the planets in our solar system will be in alignment."

Out of the corner of your eye you see that Maloder has reached the summit of the other mountain. He and his henchmen wave their arms in frustrated anger at not finding you there.

Baba Bubu starts to talk in a deep melodious voice. Everyone gives him their full attention. "The law of the universe is cause and effect. If we make good causes in our lives, we will have good effects in our lives. If we make violent causes, we will get violent effects. Violence will come back against us."

You wish Maloder and his crew could listen to this. But you wonder, did you make a bad cause? Was your desire to find the gold bringing this effect on you? Yet it wasn't greed that brought you to Peru: it was adventure, discovery—and the desire to prove that your computer program worked.

Maloder and his gang, coming down from the top of the peak, arrive at the point in the trail where you and Sally jumped. They stop and look across the chasm at the group. You hunch down into the borrowed poncho.

Turn to the next page.

"Om Shanti Om, Om Shanti Om . . ." The chanting lasts through the afternoon. The sun sets behind a peak. The last train of the day is about to leave.

You borrow Mariposa's binoculars to scan the station far below. As you focus them, Maloder springs into view. The henchman with the shaved head steps off the train, shrugging his shoulders.

Maloder looks back up toward the mountain peak. How, he must be asking himself, could they have disappeared so completely?

The train pulls out of the station, leaving Maloder and his men behind. That means they'll be in Machu Picchu at least overnight.

Turn to page 63.

42

You run to the car. The front end is held up by a jack! You push the car with all your strength. It falls off the jack and starts to coast toward the road. You jump in just in time. The tall man sprints alongside you, stretching his arm out to grab you. But the car has picked up too much speed for him to make contact. You turn the wheel sharply. The tires squeal as the old car cuts across a sharp curve onto the narrow, twisting road. As you come into the next blind corner you spot the dark blue car. You swerve to avoid it and just squeeze by. The man with the shaved head looks. He can't believe it's you!

You're barreling along at over sixty miles an hour now, down the steep road toward a hairpin turn.

Your foot searches for the brake pedal. Where is it? You steal a look down at the floor. There is no brake pedal, no clutch, nothing! No way to control the car. And it's too late to jump out! The corner comes at you, and you crank the wheel with all your strength. The car flips over and flies off the cliff. A thousand feet below is downtown Cuzco—your next and last stop.

The End

"I'll go," you say loudly and step forward.

El comandante grabs you by the arm. Remembering the satellite photo and map in your backpack, you reach for them to hand to Sally, but *el comandante* pushes you out the door.

You're led between two rows of heavily armed soldiers toward the waiting helicopter. *El comandante* presses cold metal to the back of your neck. You're sweating in the heat and with the knowledge that each step might be your last.

You and the guerrillas make it to the helicopter. They shove you in and kick the pilot out. *El comandante* takes the controls, and the helicopter rises quickly above the train and river. You feel a warmth on your thigh and look down to see the young Incan guerrilla rubbing a medicated salve on your leg. Everything goes black.

Turn to the next page.

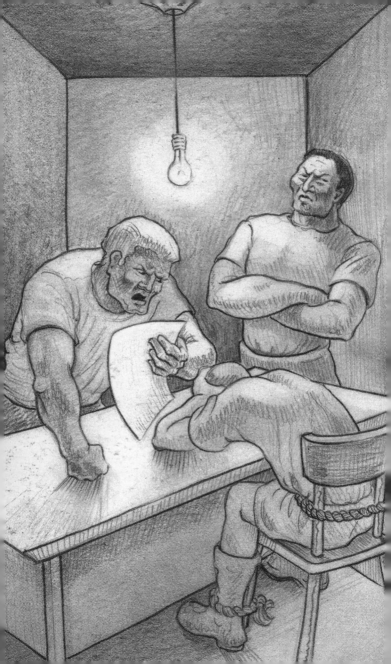

When you wake up, you realize that the powerful salve had sedated you. You look around and become aware you're tied tightly to a chair. Two very grim men sit at a table staring at you. You have no idea where you are, but it's very hot, the bare cement walls of the room drip with humidity.

"Your trial can now begin," one man says.

You straighten up in your chair, straining against the ropes. "Trial for what? What am I accused of?"

A hawklike man at the end spits out his words. "You are a spy." He holds up the satellite photo. "One more foreigner invading our land, cheating us. An example must be made."

A white-haired man speaks in a low smooth voice. "Our justice is fair. You can plead guilty or innocent. However, if you simply confess your crime here and now, I assure you we will let you go." Another man appears and points a video camera at you. "We don't care about you. All we want is your confession on tape, that is what is useful to us. That is why if you admit you are a spy, we will let you go free."

"And what if I ask for a trial and plead innocent?"

"You will receive a fair trial, of course, but you risk the death penalty if you are found guilty of spying. So quickly, what will you do?"

If you decide to "confess," turn to page 75.

If you plead innocent, turn to page 76.

If you decide to do neither, but tell them about the Lost City of Gold, turn to page 81.

You and Sally take a taxi to the Cuzco airfield. Soon, outside a hangar for private planes, a cheerful Maria fits a parachute on your back. Sally shows you the ring on your chest to pull if your chute doesn't open automatically.

"You're getting a crash course in parachuting from an expert," she says, indicating Maria. "She was always the most daring girl in our class and the best athlete."

"A crash course!" you exclaim. "You mean a quick course, I hope!"

You load all your equipment: food, radio, and survival gear, in the back of Maria's single-engine plane.

As the plane gathers speed down the runway, you notice that Paul Leduc's ominous black aircraft is gone.

Two hours later you're over the target area. Storm clouds cover the rugged terrain where you think the Lost City of Gold might be. The sun still shines on the clearing, your chosen drop zone.

Sally pushes you toward the door. "You jump first, I'll be right behind you."

You stand in the open doorway. Leaping into space goes against all your instincts.

Maria, eyeing her instruments and slowing the plane, counts down: "seven . . . six . . . five . . . four . . . three . . . two . . . one . . . JUMP!"

Go on to the nesxt page.

You fly out into space, hit by a blast of wind. You don't know if you jumped or were pushed. And your chute's not opening. Where's that ring you're supposed to pull? Where is it?

As you grope for the ring in growing panic, you're roughly jerked. Your white chute blossoms above you. It opened automatically. Two more chutes open—Sally's and the one carrying the equipment.

From the plane, the jungle had looked like a smooth green blanket. Now it's looking more and more like the back of an angry porcupine, with sharp trees for quills. As you lose altitude, you lose sight of your target, the clearing. And Sally is being blown by the storm winds farther and farther away from you. This is not the way it was supposed to go.

The jungle comes at you fast. Too fast, but there's nothing you can do. CRRRRRRRRASH!

Turn to the next page.

48

You unbuckle and fall to the ground. It's very quiet. You have your pack with some food, water, and a compass. But the satellite photo, map, and radio are in the equipment pack. It and Sally must have landed a long way from you. How can you contact each other? You should have thought to bring little walkie-talkies. Under the thick canopy of jungle you can't even see the sun. The best plan, you decide, is to make your way to the clearing where you were both supposed to land. But to do that you need to know where you are. And you don't.

Turn to the next page.

For two days you fight off the muggy embrace of the jungle. Sally and the equipment are nowhere to be found. You no longer care enough to slap at the mosquitoes that feast on exposed skin. You've never felt more alone in your life.

Through your exhaustion you hear a different sound amidst the jungle chatter. A low roar, like an engine. But it couldn't be an engine. It must be a waterfall, you decide. The very thought of quenching your thirst and finding a river way out of this "Green Hell" energizes you. You stumble on toward the noise.

The earth beneath you shakes. Above you the tops of trees shudder and abruptly disappear. An earthquake? You run and come out in a clearing. Two giant, snorting bulldozers are leveling the rain forest. Two men stand in the clearing studying a map.

Turn to page 58.

Should you jump off the roof of the train into the water? A risky jump! Yet less risky than going into a concrete wall at eighty miles an hour. And there are still at least five hostages on the train. Maybe there's a way you could stop the train in the few minutes left.

You motion to Sally to prepare to jump. The locomotive barrels onto the bridge. Seconds later, Sally leaps into the churning river below. You have a split second to decide what you'll do.

If you jump, turn to the next page.

If you stay to try to stop the train,
turn to page 99.

52

As you hurtle toward the river below, you make your body as straight as possible. Your feet punch the water with tremendous force, and you rocket to the river bottom. Pain shoots up your leg as you hit.

When you come to the surface, gasping for air, Sally is swimming near you. You start a stroke, but the pain in your leg stops you.

The army helicopter pilot has seen you, and the chopper now hovers above. A rope ladder is dropped down. It slaps the water a few feet away. You manage to grab on, even though the wind from the helicopter blade churns up waves in the icy river water.

Turn to page 9.

The next morning you and Sally leave your hotel in Cuzco at four A.M. and crowd into an old bus packed with Indians, chickens, baby pigs, and sacks of potatoes and various herbs. Your equipment for the expedition is secured on top, along with a number of passengers who couldn't afford the luxury of seats.

Shivering in your bus seat on your way to Soledad, you happily watch the morning sun clear the snow-covered Andes. You feel the warmth on your face and better understand why the Incas worshipped the sun in this cold, high-altitude world.

You're pretty confident that you aren't being followed. Maloder and his men would never have expected you to take an ancient, rickety bus over the mighty Andes. Your destination is the jungle river town of Tres Cruces, but you have a long trip ahead of you before you descend the eastern slopes of the Andean range into the Amazon Basin.

Turn to the next page.

56

The bus has labored all day to climb the endless switchback roads. At this altitude the landscape is barren and vast. From time to time you pass groups of Andean Indians, often with herds of llamas.

At sunset you come into a town nestled on a pass—the halfway point of your trip, before the road plunges down into the jungles of the Amazon Basin.

The bus limps into the main plaza. A fiesta is in full swing. Brass bands play the haunting marches of the high-altitude Indian. Nearly everyone is in bright costumes with terrifying masks. Everyone seems to stagger, exhausted from days of celebration.

You ask the driver how long the stopover will be, but he only shrugs his shoulders.

"Una hora?" you inquire in your best Spanish.

He seems to indicate longer, but he and everyone else pile out of the bus.

The bus could remain in the small town all night—or the driver could start it up again in an hour's time. It's chancy to let the bus out of your sight. But observing the ancient rites of the fiesta might give you new insight into the ancient Incas.

If you decide to check out the fiesta, turn to page 61.

If you decide to stay on the bus, turn to page 69.

Your quest for the Lost City of Gold must continue, so the next morning, you bid a sad good-bye to Kalotaxidi. Sally and you owe him your lives. He refuses to accept any gifts, even your pocket knife.

After a hard morning's hike, you break to eat some of your rations. Sally sets up the equipment to get a fix on your position from a navigational satellite overhead. Finding your way in the jungle is much like being fogbound on the ocean. The sun is rarely visible under the tropical canopy and, as on the open sea, there are no landmarks by which to double-check your position.

"We're only five and a-quarter miles away," Sally reports. Your heart quickens with excitement.

That evening you make camp less than half a mile from your goal—the straight line on your computer screen and the clearing on your satellite photo. Even though you're tired, you have trouble going to sleep. What will be there? Will you find the ancient Inca Lost City of Gold? Tomorrow morning you'll know the answer. Will you make the greatest archaeological discovery of your time? Or will you find nothing?

Turn to page 108.

58

Something suddenly makes you look behind you. Standing there like a mirage is an Indian with a painted face, feathers in his straight black hair. He carries a bow and arrow, and beckons you to come back into the jungle. You ignore him and turn back to the workers and the machines. They can bring you back to civilization.

The Indian holds up a red bandanna. It's Sally's! You hesitate. The Indian seems to point to the bulldozers and draws his hand across his throat in a cutting motion. Does he mean Sally has been killed? Does he mean he'll kill you if you go to the men clearing the jungle? Or is he trying to warn you that the workers will kill you? What should you do?

If you decide to follow the Indian, turn to page 64.

If you decide to approach the men working, turn to page 77.

You and Sally step down from the bus and are swept away in the dense crowd. Half the revelers are dancing; the multicolored skirts of the women swirl in circles of color. You take some photographs with your camera, though the people don't seem to like it.

In the shadows of early evening, you find yourself separated from Sally at the edge of the crowd. You smell incense and candles burning and spot a llama, wearing streamers, lying on the ground as some forty people sing softly around it. You take some pictures before you realize that the llama is about to be sacrificed. The two Indians serving as priests in this ancient Incan ritual will scatter the llama's blood on *Pacha Mama,* Mother Earth, so the coming harvest will be bountiful.

A young child sees your camera, points at you, and calls out. Suddenly the whole crowd is staring at you. They start shouting angrily. You run, but they catch you. It's the young child who throws the first stone.

Turn to the next page.

62

The doctors in the Cuzco hospital do a good job on your injuries. A kindly woman doctor tells you that what you did was very foolish and disrespectful. "Many people on this earth believe you are capturing their soul when you take a photograph. You really were stealing something from them, and the least you could have done was ask permission."

One day Sally visits and tells you the good news that you can fly home in a few days. The bad news is that you still have a long convalescence ahead.

The End

Baba Bubu sounds his gong again. "We will break into two groups to prepare for possible miracles at this crucial moment for Mother Earth. Those who wish to do past-life regression will go with Mariposa; those who wish to do levitation, stay here."

Past-life regression? Levitation? Mariposa senses your uncertainty. "When I do past-life regression, I hypnotize you and take you back into your past lives."

"Past lives?" Sally asks.

"Yes. We believe that our souls are eternal, they come back through many lifetimes. We can learn much from this. I lived a fascinating past life in ancient Egypt." She looks at you with piercing but kind eyes. "Perhaps in a past life you were an Inca. Sitting on a golden throne."

That does sound interesting. Maybe you're fulfilling your destiny by discovering the Lost City of Gold in this lifetime. Maybe you could find out where it is by going into a past life. But being hypnotized could be dangerous, especially if Maloder shows up.

"And what about levitation?" You question.

"If you concentrate and chant, you can float off the ground." Mariposa explains. I have seen it in India, and maybe now in this special moment, you can do it."

If you want to try going back into a past life, turn to page 94.

If you want to try levitation, turn to page 103.

64

The Indian turns as you go toward him. He moves effortlessly through the thick vegetation. You struggle to keep up. All efforts to communicate with him by sign language are answered by a brisk movement of his hand indicating you should move faster.

At evening, you smell something different in the dark jungle air. Smoke. A fire means you must be coming close to a village. Your spirits pick up.

The Indian leads you into a clearing by a stream. A single figure bends over a fire, cooking a fish on a forked stick. It's Sally.

You joyfully embrace.

"We've sure come a long way from the university computer room," you tell Sally. "Did you find the other parachute?"

"Yes, it fell near me. The radio works, and everything else is fine."

"Are we near the site?" you ask, once again interested in the Lost City of Gold.

"Yes, but Kalotaxidi here wants us to come to his adopted village. He says he'll show us something better than gold."

"How did you find that out? And how do you know his name?" you ask. The Indian never spoke to you.

Go on to the next page.

You're surprised when Kalotaxidi himself breaks his silence.

"Words cannot be trusted with strangers. We were strangers when we met in the jungle. Now we are friends," Kalotaxidi answers in English. "Come with me, my new companions, and you will go to a world that words can never describe."

If you decide to go with Kalotaxidi, turn to page 104.

If you decide to search for the Lost City of Gold, turn to page 57.

66

You set off with Sally in the direction of the river as though your lives depend on it, which they may. After a few days, your only goal in life is just to put one foot ahead of the other. Decisions become very basic. Should you take off your shoes to get rid of the ants that are biting at you. Or, should you leave them on, knowing that if you expose your bare feet, the mosquitoes will attack your feet, leaving them numb and swollen?

Finally you make it to the river, and with what strength the two of you have left, you construct a crude raft. Your map shows that this river leads into the Amazon and, some four thousand miles later, flows into the Atlantic Ocean.

Days go by on the raft. You're feverish with the heat, and Sally is sick with malaria. And your food supply has run out. The irony is that your small, shortwave radio works, but the batteries aren't strong enough for your two-way radio. You can hear London, Tokyo, New York, learn all the news of the world, but the world knows nothing of you.

Days and nights fold one into the other. The last thing you remember, as you drift off once more into unconsciousness is hearing a voice with a British accent, just more BBC news.

Go on to the next page.

You grow dimly aware of voices calling. You open your eyes, and through a haze, you see two concerned faces. Maybe the voices aren't coming from the radio. You blink your eyes. The haze is a mosquito net. The faces look like your next-door neighbors'. Are you back home?

"Can you hear me now?" a blond-bearded man asks softly.

"Yes. Where's Sally?"

"She's fine."

"Where are we?"

"You're at a missionaries' clinic in Santa Rosa," he answers.

Sally joins the other two faces at the netting over your bed. She looks thin and very sunburned, but she's smiling.

In a few days you're flown from the jungle landing strip to Cuzco, and from there on home. One thing you know is that if you go on another adventure, you're going to go where there's snow—never again to the furnace of the "Green Hell".

The End

You and Sally renew your search for the Lost City of Gold by heading toward higher ground. A cloud covers the area above you. You notice that there's also a cloud over that area on your satellite photo.

You set off climbing, following what seems to be a natural trail. But soon you come up against a cliff. A dead end. There are vines on the cliff though, and you wonder if you can climb them. You grab onto one of the vines and start to climb. Uh-oh! You feel the vine pull free, and you go crashing to the ground.

"Look here!" Sally yells. She's pointing to where the vine had covered the face of the cliff. Steps cut into the rock zigzag toward the top of the cliff. You and Sally quickly scramble up.

On top, you see a path overgrown with moss. Under the moss are flat stones set in the Inca style. You're on one of the old Inca highways that linked the far reaches of the empire. Runners used these roads to carry messages which were conveyed by colored strings called *khipu*.

Walking is now easy along the road. Your excitement grows; you know this highway will lead to something. Up ahead you can see the steep face of a mountain.

Turn to page 114.

You and Sally wait on the bus while the other passengers climb out onto the plaza. Luckily, the driver returns about forty-five minutes later and starts up the bus.

You travel all night, and by mid-morning of the following day, the bus has reached the end of the road. You entered the small river town of Tres Cruces. You and Sally stumble out. You're stiff and beaten up from all the bouncing on the rough dirt roads. Not having slept all night, you'd welcome nothing more than a nice comfortable bed.

Your bags are thrown down from the bus into the middle of the road. Unlike in Cuzco, where scores of kids rushed to help you with your bags, everyone seems asleep in the hot, steamy river town.

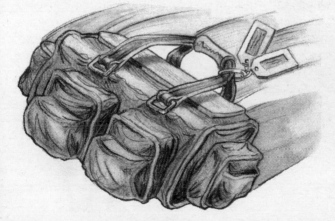

Turn to the next page.

You stagger into a hotel with your bags. An unshaven man is asleep at the desk. When you ring the little bell next to him, he opens an eye.

"What are you doing here?" he asks in a sour tone.

"We'd like two rooms, *por favor,*" you answer.

The man stands up with great effort, revealing an enormous stomach. He's shirtless and sweating in rivulets.

"You are not tourists," he says. You look at him for some explanation. "Tourists never come here. Only fortune hunters and fugitives do, and you don't look like criminals fleeing the law."

You say nothing. You take your key and hand Sally hers.

"If you are fortune hunters, you'll need a boat. And if you need a boat, you have to see the twins. They not only know everything, they control everything here."

"The twins?"

"Yes, you are in luck. They both are here today." The fat man looks at you from under half-closed eyes. "Be careful! One of them always lies and the other one always tells the truth. Sometimes they say nothing at all."

"Which one tells the truth?" you ask hopefully.

The fat man bursts out laughing. His two front teeth are shining gold. He says nothing more.

Go on to the next page.

You walk into an open-air room at the back of the hotel, where two men are sitting. When the hotel owner said "twins," you expected them to be identical. But these men look completely different.

They stand as you and Sally enter, beckoning you to join them. One of them is dressed in a spotless white suit, wears a Panama hat, and is freshly shaven. The other is bearded, with tousled hair. He clearly has no interest in his appearance. They look you over as you sit down. And you look them over. Suddenly you realize they are identical twins, but they present themselves to the world in completely different ways.

You decide to be very direct. "Do you always tell the truth?" you ask the twin in the white suit.

"Yes, I do," he replies in an insulted tone.

You turn to the wild-looking one. "Do you always tell the truth?"

"Yes, I do," the wild one answers. "Do you?"

"Yes," you say with some hesitation.

"Well then, answer me this. Have you come to Tres Cruces seeking the Lost City of Gold? And if so, why here? You must have knowledge others don't. A map, perhaps?"

Turn to the next page.

Does he know about the satellite photo or is he just guessing, you wonder. Maybe he knows Maloder, too.

Trying not to reveal anything, you say, "I believe I was asking the questions." And you turn to the twin in the white suit. "Does your brother always lie?"

"Yes, he does," the neat man answers.

"What is your name?" you ask the messy brother.

"Hernando de Soto," he replies.

"And what is your name?" you ask the brother in the impeccable white suit.

"Hernando de Soto," this brother also replies.

Turn to the next page.

Sally decides to test them. "Does two plus two equal five?" she asks the unshaven brother. The twins are silent. You realize the hotel clerk was right—they will answer only the questions they choose.

You ask them every question you can think of, but you can't figure out which one is telling the truth. They think it's all very funny.

Suddenly the man in the white suit stops laughing. "If you are here for gold, I can help you," he says. "There is no Lost City of Gold. That is all a legend. The Incas dumped the gold into a lake, and I can show you where it is. But if I show you, you must agree to pay me fifty percent of all the gold you recover from the lake."

"Don't believe him," his brother says sharply. "There is a Lost City of Gold, and I will show it to you, but on one condition."

"What is the condition?" you ask with some suspicion.

"First, you must decide whether to trust me or my brother. If you choose me, I will tell you the condition. Otherwise I will not tell you, nor will I show you the Lost City of Gold."

If you decide to go with the perfectly dressed twin to the lake, turn to page 84.

If you decide to trust his brother, without knowing his condition, turn to page 83.

"I'll confess," you say, and one of the guerrillas quickly unties you.

The man with the video camera moves closer and says, "Repeat that!"

"I confess. I'm guilty," you say again.

"What? Speak up, we can not hear you."

"Guilty." You say it a third time, without any conviction. You hope anyone watching the video-tape will know your "confession" is false.

You stand up to leave.

Two guerrilla guards appear from the dark corners of the room. They tie your hands.

"What is this?" you protest "You promised that all you wanted was a statement and you would let me go free."

"But you are guilty! You yourself have said so. Take this criminal away!"

As you face the firing squad, you have one last thought. If only you had chosen to plead innocent, then you might remain alive, free to find the Lost City of Gold, to be rich and famous . . .

The End

"I'm innocent!" you say. You don't trust them, and it's better to tell the truth.

"You are lying! We have the evidence!" shouts the white-haired man.

"You are guilty! We will vote. All those in favor of guilty raise their hands!"

"But," you protest, "I must have the chance to plead my case. Have a lawyer."

"We do not have time to waste."

Two hands go up, and the two look at the third "judge" with surprise.

"Are you asleep? We are voting," demands the white-haired guerrilla with irritation.

"No, I hate unanimous votes, they are so boring."

"Guilty, then, two votes to one, take the prisoner away!"

You're led outside to a wall, an ancient Inca wall of perfectly fitted massive stones. You look up toward eight guerrillas raising their rifles.

"Do you want a blindfold?" asks *el comandante.*

"No."

"Ready . . . Aim—."

Your last thought is of how stupid you were not to "confess" and be let free.

The End

You rush toward the two men bent over the map. "Hello! Hello!" you call. The sound of the bulldozers is too loud for them to hear you until you're at their side. "I'm so glad that I found you," you yell. "I need help. My friend's lost out there."

Their surprise at seeing you turns to suspicion. "What are you doing here?"

"I'm an archaeologist," you reply.

"We have a road to build," announces one of the workers, a tall bushy-haired man in a safari suit. "But Herman here will call in on the radio."

A few hours later a helicopter descends from the sky. As you walk toward it, you notice a golden puma with emerald eyes painted on the fuselage. That's Paul Leduc's insignia! With growing dread you now see the emblem on the bulldozers, too. The pilot holds the door open for you. You know that if you run back into the jungle you have no chance of surviving. As dangerous as Paul Leduc may be, flying out of here in his helicopter is your only chance. You step into the aircraft.

Turn to the next page.

After a half hour, the pilot lands in a cleared section of the jungle. You see several buildings: long sheds, huts, an impressive main house, as well as a hangar and an airstrip. Your heart sinks as you spot Leduc's black aircraft parked by the hangar.

So far, you've been treated as a guest. You hope Paul Leduc will help you rescue Sally from the jungle.

A very polite servant leads you to a tidy guest house. You find formal evening clothes laid out on the bed. As you dress, you decide to ask your host to mount an immediate search for Sally.

Escorted to the main house, you enter a large dining room, where thirteen people sit, eight men and five women, all elegantly dressed. The man at the head of the table rises.

It's Paul Leduc. "It is an honor to have you among us," he says. "I know of your brilliant work." A giant Doberman stands by his side.

The guests study you strangely, making comments: "Very fit. Strong." "A swift runner, I'll wager." "And certainly clever."

"This is my hunting lodge, and these are my business associates," Leduc explains. "We have come in quest of the ultimate hunting challenge."

Turn to the next page.

80

"What do you hunt?" you inquire with real curiosity.

The guests look at each other and smirk. "We hunt the most dangerous quarry of all," one of them answers. "An animal which knows the terrain perfectly, a killer at fifty yards, intelligent and deadly."

You wonder what ferocious beast that could be.

Turn to page 124.

"I am an archaeologist, not a spy," you say quietly. "That map shows where the Incas' Lost City of Gold is, where the royal treasury of gold and silver was hidden from the Spanish."

"This is all a fairy tale!" shouts the hawk-faced man.

You go on, "And in that treasure is the great golden throne of the last Inca."

The white-haired man looks down at the satellite photo. "What if it's true? Can you imagine if I sat on the golden throne of the last Inca? Every Indian in the mountains would rise against the outsiders. The prophecy of the Incas' return would be fulfilled."

The others are now enthusiastic, but they need you to interpret the photo.

"And if I lead you there," you speak up, "what will be my reward?"

"We will spare your life. You have our word. As the Inca."

Turn to the next page.

By the second day of your trip into the jungles of the Soledad region, the guerrillas are so fired up with visions of gold and new Inca power that they pay little attention to you. You, too, are excited with the possibility of discovering the Lost City of Gold, but you don't want to help them. And what if the straight line shown by your computer analysis turns out to be nothing? The guerrillas won't treat you too kindly then.

That night you disappear into the jungle.

Within a week you've returned back home. You scan the newspapers every day for news of a discovery or news of a guerrilla action, but there's nothing.

Some months later, you scan a new batch of NASA satellite photos of the Soledad region. There, in the area of the straight line, you see that much clearing has been done, revealing the ruins of buildings. The city is there! Have the guerrillas uncovered the ruins? Or has someone else found the city? And is it the Lost City of Gold? Maybe one day you'll make another expedition back to find out.

The End

"You accept my unnamed condition, then," says the unshaven brother after you agree to trust him.

The twin in the white suit shrugs his shoulders and stands up to leave. "I am sorry for you, my young friends. You chose a liar." He walks out leaving you alone with his brother.

"So, I will take you to see the treasure of the Incas. My condition is that you promise you will let it stay where it is. I say this mainly for your own good. All those who have tried to remove the treasure have come to a terrible end. The treasure of the Incas is cursed."

You never guessed this would be his condition. What is he up to? Is he telling the truth about the curse?

He sees your look of suspicion. "I sensed that you are the kind of people who did not come here for greed, but came to satisfy your curiosity that the treasure exists. Won't just seeing it be enough?"

Turn to page 88.

When you say you'll go with the white-suited twin, he grins. You and Sally follow him to a dock and step aboard his luxurious riverboat. Asking for fifty percent of the gold sounded like a serious business proposition. At least you know where you stand with this twin. You hope.

The trip on the river lasts three days. You and Sally spend most of the time reading and talking to the crew of the twin's riverboat.

On the third day, after the boat has docked, you, Sally, the twin, and half the crew members trek overland for another two days. You all climb up to the top of a small volcano, and there, three hundred feet below, is a clear, circular lake. Even from there, you can see a gold glint under the water. You're so excited you could jump right into the crater.

"There really is gold here, Hernando, you were telling the truth!" you exclaim.

"I always tell the truth." He smiles. "Go ahead. Go see for yourself," he urges. "Leave your backpack here."

"Señor Carlos, I will help him," says one of the crew members as he comes forward to take your pack.

You and Sally rush down the steep slope, but you're slowed as your feet sink deeply into the soft volcanic soil.

The closer you get to the lake the more the gold seems to glimmer beneath the water.

Turn to the next page.

86

You and Sally dive into the clear water and stroke down toward the glint. Just when it feels as if your lungs will burst, you reach a glimmering rock, grab it, and shoot back to the surface.

Gasping for breath you examine the rock eagerly.

You know right away—it's mica. Fool's gold!

A shadow passes over you. You look up to see a black cloud and feel raindrops in your face. Suddenly the sky breaks open and you are drenched with rain. Peals of laughter echo around the crater. You see Hernando. No, wait! One of the crew members had called him Carlos! He was lying. Lying to you about his name and the location of the gold. And you realize that now he has the satellite photo, and the map you left behind in your backpack. You suspected the wrong twin of knowing Maloder.

Go on to the next page.

You and Sally try to climb up the steep side of the crater, but you slide back. And the downpour is making it more slippery by the minute. Tumbling down to the lake's edge in total exhaustion, you notice bones for the first time. Human bones.

Sally still has her backpack, but—except for one candy bar—all the food supplies were in your pack. You hang on for days. So does the rain. Once you nearly make it to the top, only to fall back again. Without food you grow weaker and weaker. Sally's miniature shortwave radio is small comfort. When finally you're too weak to move, you hear a faint broadcast. The announcer reports that the greatest archaeological find of the century has been discovered in Peru by Paul Leduc. You only hope that Sally will make it out alive—unlike you.

The End

"Yes," you say, without much enthusiasm. If he's going to take you there, then of course you'll know how to go back. And you must go back to document your find. An archaeological discovery as important as this one must not be kept secret. Perhaps he's a trusting person, the brother who tells the truth. So far you don't see that he's taking unfair advantage of you in any way.

"So, it is a long way. You must get a good night's sleep. We will leave in the morning." As he walks away, he turns and says, "By the way, you will be blindfolded during the trip. You understand of course."

Go on to the next page.

That evening, you and Sally take a stroll around the decaying town. At a small shop, you buy a necklace with hundreds of shiny little black beads.

"I didn't know you were interested in jewelry," Sally says with playful surprise. You're too preoccupied to answer.

"Sally, if this is the twin who's lying, he might have some horrible end in store for us. It's better I go alone. If I don't come back, you can get help and come looking for me."

Sally agrees. Your plan makes sense.

The twin shows up in the hotel at daybreak. Luckily he doesn't ask why Sally hasn't come along. He puts the blindfold on you at the edge of the village.

The trip is long. For the first half you ride on the back of a mule, then later, you walk. At night you camp out, and you're too tired to think about a way to take off the blindfold without the twin catching you.

Turn to the next page.

The next day you're led through a much cooler area, probably a building or cave.

Here the twin removes the blindfold. It's pitch-black. A torch is lit, and a fabulous golden treasure comes to life before your eyes!

"Yes, my friend, this is the Lost City of Gold. The Incas brought it all here, and here is where it must stay," Hernando states.

"May I take a photo?" you ask pulling out your digital camera. He nods, and you take one photo and quickly put the camera in your pocket.

The blindfold is put back on for the return journey. You reach into your other pocket, where you have the necklace, and secretly drop a bead every few hundred feet on the trail.

Turn to the next page.

The next morning Hernando drops you off at the hotel. You excitedly tell Sally about what you've seen.

"Oh, I envy you so much, I'd love to see the treasure."

"You can," you answer confidently.

"But how? You were blindfolded," Sally says.

"I marked the trail with the beads from that necklace I bought."

"Oh, I'm not sure that's right," Sally says. "Hernando's the honest twin, and you agreed to his condition."

"Yes, the condition was to leave the gold just as it is. We're only going to look and take more pictures," you reply.

"Okay," Sally says, "but I'm not sure I feel right about it, especially if we show the pictures to others."

Go on to the next page.

The next day you set out, searching for the trail. You spend all day on the only two possible trails out of town, but you don't find a single black bead.

Remembering the photo you took, you go back to the hotel. You grab the digital camera and turn it on. The photo that appears on the screen is dark and blurry. Could it all have been a dream? No, you have the images of the treasure in your mind, you'll just have to look harder for those beads.

Downstairs, in the hotel lobby, Hernando greets you. He hands you an envelope. "Hello, my friend, I think you must have lost these!"

Puzzled, you open the envelope. It's full of shiny black beads.

The End

You and Sally climb with the past-life regression group to the peak of the mountain. Mariposa leads you to a sheltered place to sit amidst the rocks.

"Relax. Take some deep breaths." She takes a golden locket from around her neck. Holding the chain between her fingers, she swings the locket back and forth like a pendulum. "Just watch the locket. Back and forth. That's right."

You concentrate on the shiny gold object. Back and forth. You feel drowsy. Back and forth.

Mariposa's voice is very soothing. "You are a cloud. A fluffy white cloud floating in an endless blue sky."

Go on to the next page.

Crack! A branch slaps across your face. You're walking in a jungle. You look down at your body. You're dressed in clothes made of a shiny material you've never seen. Your body is very cool in these clothes, though you feel the torrid heat of the jungle on your exposed face.

Behind you are your companions, two men dressed in the same kind of bizarre glossy outfits.

"Zop it," says the shorter man. The language he speaks sounds like English, yet it's not familiar. He pulls out what appears to be a map, but it's in three dimensions. A red point of light seems to indicate where you are.

The clothes, the language, the map, how can you explain them? You've never read anything like this in history books.

Turn to the next page.

96

After a long winding climb, you and your companions come to a narrow pass in a hillside. Looking down at your feet, you see the flat large stones of an Inca road.

Once through the pass, a natural gateway, you face a wall of thick vegetation. One of the men draws what looks like a gun and points it at the wall. The plants retreat. They grow in reverse, shrinking, to disappear in the ground. Before you is an impressive wall, with a gate leading to a passageway through the wall.

Walking through the passageway, illuminated by slits in the ceiling, you come into a vast chamber. Time has clogged the chamber with moss and vines. Again the amazing gun is brought into play. The plants retreat to reveal a magnificent treasure.

At the far end is the golden throne of the last Inca, encrusted with emeralds. Statues in gold of faithful retainers line the walls. And at the side of the throne, a golden puma with piercing green eyes. You've found the Lost City of Gold!

There's only one explanation. Your clothes, the incredible gun—you must be from another planet. But is this life in your past—or your future?

You hear a growl above you. You look up as a jaguar leaps through the air, his teeth and claws aimed at your throat. You scream.

Turn to page 125.

You head toward the main house, sloshing through streams to throw the dogs off the scent. You reach the far end of the settlement just as a pistol shot and the loud yipping of dogs signal the beginning of the hunt. The barking recedes as the dogs tear off into the tropical forest hot on your trail.

Seeing no one around, you dash across the clearing to a large thatched building. The door is open and you duck inside.

Suddenly you hear voices approaching. Where can you hide? Inside the hut are several enormous steel vats. You quickly climb up over the side of one and tumble inside.

You hear some men enter the hut, then quickly leave. As you begin to climb out of the vat, a terrible smell assaults your nostrils. The fumes start to make you dizzy, and you fall back into the vat—which will soon become your tomb.

The End

Lying flat on the roof, you see Sally knife cleanly into the river. Then the train shoots under an overpass, and the river is blotted from view. You don't know if she came to the surface or not.

Bent against the onrushing wind from the train's high speed, you move toward the head of the train. You drop down onto the platform of the next car. From there, you see that the young Incan guerrilla is holding the frightened people hostage in the last car.

Dropping to your knees, you see that a large steel pin holds the two cars together. City buildings now whip by. Cuzco! You reach down, brace your legs, and with all your strength, pull on the pin. It comes out. The last car, now unhitched from the rest of the train, starts to drift away from you. The young guerrilla, sensing something has happened, runs to the door.

The uncoupled car slows almost to a stop. Apparently the young guerrilla is a quick thinker, because, before you turn away, you see him climbing off the train. The hostages are safe. But you're not.

You open the door into the railway car. The car's empty. There must be an emergency brake somewhere, you think. You've only got seconds left.

Turn to the next page.

You run forward. The car is swaying so much at the high speed that it's nearly impossible to keep your balance.

You make it to the door that leads to the locomotive. The guerrilla leader is alone in the locomotive cabin, his right hand gripping the throttle. You pull on the door, but it won't open. You bang on it. *El comandante* turns around. His eyes and face are wild. He's a man possessed; nothing will stop him.

You look back, up, down. There's something! A red handle. Behind a pane of glass on the wall. You smash the glass, grip the handle, and pull with all your strength. You're launched forward with the velocity of a popcorn off a hot griddle. Luckily, you hit a padded seat.

The train wheels have locked. The steel wheels grinding on the tracks send up a shower of sparks as the train hurtles into the station. Waiting passengers and street vendors scatter in panic.

You're thrown against the seat once more as the locomotive breaks through the metal guard at the end of the tracks and comes to rest against the far wall of the station.

There's a moment of unnatural silence. Then screams, and the sounds of people rushing toward the crippled train.

Turn to the next page.

You're a hero. You still don't understand what made you do what you did, but you saved many lives.

Sally and you are flown to Lima, the capital of Peru, where the President of the Republic awards you a special medal. Your picture appears in all the newspapers of the world. And that's not all. A television cameraman in the army helicopter not only filmed Sally's dive into the river, he also captured your mad dash along the roof of the train. The whole world has watched your bravery.

The End

Sally goes off with Mariposa, while you stay behind with the group doing levitation.

For hours you concentrate deep within yourself, your eyes firmly shut. You feel the life force within you surging upward, pushing against the force of gravity which presses down on you. You focus all your energy on imagining your body floating off the ground.

Suddenly you feel yourself rising— you no longer feel the ground under you! It is as if a number of strong hands are lifting you up. It's a miracle! You smile at yourself. You really didn't believe it was possible. Though you realize that doing so might spoil the miracle, you have to open your eyes.

There before you is another smiling face. Maloder's. His two thugs have lifted you up, have moved you away from the others concentrating on levitation, and are carrying you to the edge of the precipice. Maloder takes your backpack, gleefully pulling out the satellite photo and map.

"You can't do this! It's against the law. It's murder!" you cry out.

"The only law I know is gravity. What goes up must come down," Professor Maloder calmly replies.

They throw you off the mountain. Down is two thousand feet.

The End

104

You, Sally, and Kalotaxidi travel for some days toward his adopted village. With each day that passes you feel more at home. Somehow the nightmare of heat and bugs fades, and the jungle becomes more and more magical.

At last you come to a broad river. Kalotaxidi retrieves his pirogue, a boat carved out of a large tree trunk, and you all climb aboard. The current takes you gently along. Kalotaxidi disappears from time to time to hunt, coming back with birds, a monkey, a wild boar. He tells you that these are for a feast that will take place upon arrival at his village.

You hear the sound of drums as you approach a bend in the river. You've reached the village.

Kalotaxidi is greeted at the riverbank by excited villagers decorated for the feast with bright paints and brilliant feathers. They make appreciative sounds as each piece of game is taken from the pirogue. But their greatest surprise and wonder is over you and Sally.

You're led to a hut in the middle of the village. Kalotaxidi invites you to join the circle of people sitting on the floor of the hut around the fire. You hesitate, but through his eyes and his gestures he indicates you will experience something magical, something you have never experienced before.

Turn to page 116.

At sunup you're led to the edge of the jungle. A pack of hunting dogs strain at their leashes.

"I will give you an hour's head start. That should be enough time for us to have a relaxed breakfast." Leduc takes a pistol from his holster and fires it into the air. "GO!"

You sprint off into the jungle. Don't panic, you tell yourself, think carefully. Should you run as far as you can into the jungle or should you double back and hide in one of the buildings?

If you decide to run into the jungle,
turn to page 98.

If you decide to double back, turn to page 111.

You and Sally are up and on the move at dawn. Crashing through the dense undergrowth, you burst into a clearing. There are stones ahead of you. A crumbling wall, but man-made! You drop your packs and run.

"Oh, no!" you exclaim, crushed with disappointment. The structure is nothing more than a low stone wall that leads nowhere. "Perhaps this was a farm that fed people in the city," you say without real hope. "Are you sure this is the right place?" you add.

"There's no doubt about it." Sally sinks to the ground.

You both hear the sound of a plane at the same moment. Maria! Sally scrambles for the radio. You wave your shirt.

"Oh, no! The batteries have gone dead! I must have left it on." she says desperately as the plane disappears, leaving only silence behind.

Turn to the next page.

110

Sally spreads the food rations out on the ground and studies the map. "If we leave now we'll have enough food to make it to this river. After that, there will only be a two- or three-day supply."

"But maybe the Lost City of Gold is nearby. We've come all this way, we could keep searching. Maria might fly over again. She'll drop food. If not, we could live off the land." Your voice reveals how unsure you are of what to do. But you have to make a choice.

If you decide to get out to safety,
turn to page 114.

If you decide to continue searching for the
Lost City of Gold, turn to page 115.

You run for your life through the jungle. The heat is stifling, and the jungle grows thicker and thicker. In the distance you hear the dogs. Each bark spurs you on.

Your senses are super alert, like those of any hunted animal. A branch moves behind you. Is it a snake? Could a dog have caught up so fast? You slowly turn. It's an Indian, blending almost perfectly with the jungle foliage. It's the man you saw near the bulldozed clearing earlier!

Once again he beckons you to follow him. This time you don't hesitate—and he swiftly leads you to a remote part of the jungle. Without him you surely would have been caught.

For days you follow your mysterious guide, communicating with him through sign language. You marvel at how at home he is in this environment, which for you is torture.

On the seventh day you're so tired you speak aloud rather than by using sign language.

To your total surprise, the Indian answers you in English spoken with an American southern accent. "I learned English from missionaries who came to teach my tribe the Bible," he explains. "Almost all of my tribe died of a disease the missionaries brought with them."

"Why do you help me, when outsiders have brought you such misery?" you ask.

"There are good and bad people of every tribe in the world. I can see that you are a good person. My name, by the way, is Kalotaxidi."

Turn to page 66.

You climb steadily for two days. The cooler air is a welcome compensation for the straining effort of climbing. Kalotaxidi follows a definite trail until he comes to a suspension bridge made of vines, which stretches across a deep ravine.

Once you've both made it safely across, Kalotaxidi calls out. Children come running, followed by adults. They're dressed like ancient Incas. And with them is Sally!

You and Sally hug with joy and relief.

"Is this the Lost City of Gold?" you ask in total wonder.

"No, not at all," Sally replies as she picks up a small Inca child who has tripped. "These are real Incas, who, aside from Kalotaxidi, never had

contact with the Spanish or anyone from the outside world. The Spanish for them are a legend. They live very peacefully."

Sally leads you to the village. The stonework and the buildings look like Machu Picchu and other Indian ruins, but this is a living village, the stone buildings covered with thatched roofs. Sally leads you to a tiny temple in the center of the settlement. Gold objects adorn the room!

She takes you next door, where men busily work crafting gold goblets. Two Inca boys furiously pump the bellows of a kiln melting gold. "No ancient treasure was brought to this refuge. They made all this here over the last few centuries."

Turn to page 121.

114

The ancient highway passes straight through a narrow gap in the mountain. Once through the gap, the road opens again into a small valley. You can see how easy it would be to defend the valley by closing off this narrow entrance way.

And there before you are Inca stone buildings. They're covered with vines and plants, but there's no doubt that what you're looking at was once a city. Broad earthen terraces, now collapsed, once stepped proudly up the mountainsides. Crops, mostly corn, were once planted there and must have fed thousands of people.

You feel this is it, this is the place you've been looking for.

"Maybe someone still lives here," Sally says.

You move through various chambers, lighting your way with a torch. They're like a maze, but finally you find yourself on the threshold of the main temple. If there's a treasure room, this is where you'll find it. But have thieves beaten you to the treasure? You wonder.

All the reading you've done and all the fantasies of your daydreams have not prepared you for the splendor of the reality. The treasure room is full of the most extraordinary ancient objects in gold and silver. A throne encrusted with emeralds. Golden figures of men and women and children. Elegant vases. Jewelry. Baths with golden basins like swimming pools fed by silver conduits. It goes on and on. You've found it! The Lost City of Gold!

Turn to page 119.

The people in the circle sway back and forth to the rhythm of a drum and the clear voice of a child singing. You, too, begin to sway back and forth, and without willing it at all or knowing the words, you find you're joining in the song.

The faces in front of you look as if they're reflected in water, water that has been disturbed. The faces flow into different shapes, then they fade.

You're looking from above down into the village. You see the main hut with smoke seeping out of its thatched roof. You're falling! Right

toward the hut, no, you're stopping, you're over the hut, you're going up, up. You're flying!

Flying! This is fantastic. You're free, nothing can hold you down. You realize you're a bird, you can see your wings. You fly as fast as you can, you dive, you climb, you love it. Below you is an opening in the jungle in a valley. You swoop down to get a closer look. Nothing but large stones in a geometric pattern. Stones don't interest you as a bird. Even shiny yellow metal doesn't interest you.

Turn to the next page.

118

You soar above the village by the river, then go into a steep dive straight at the river.

In the water you see distorted faces, but as the water grows still, you recognize those who were in the hut with you. You realize you're back in the hut. You touch your arms, half expecting to feel feathers. Sally sits across from you, her face painted with vivid red streaks. You smile and everyone in the hut smiles with you.

"How was it?" Sally asks.

"Incredible. It was real. I really was flying. But at the same time I felt I was part of everything, the water, the trees, the sky."

"I felt that as well. I was a deer." Sally grins at you and you grin back. "We took a trip within ourselves. The real adventure is inside us, isn't it?"

"Yes," you say. "I guess it doesn't matter if we find the Lost City of Gold or not, does it? We have gone to a richer kingdom in our imaginations. Or maybe we didn't imagine it. I think I really flew."

Kalotaxidi smiles. He knows that at least on your search you have found joy, a joy from within.

The End

After many hours, you and Sally emerge for fresh air. You step out into what was once the main square of this Inca stronghold. You realize finding the treasure is only half the battle—now you must get out alive to tell about it.

That afternoon you hear the sound of a plane engine. Your radio batteries had become very weak with the jungle humidity, but in this cooler place they give just enough power. Just as you hoped, your radio signal is answered by Maria. She locks in on your signal and soon slips in under the permanent cloud cover that prevents anyone from sighting the ruin from the air.

Maria drops supplies to you and flies off. The next day, a helicopter arrives and you're ferried out. You take with you a few small gold objects to show the outside world.

Turn to the next page.

120

In the capital, Lima, you hold a press conference at the National Archaeological Association of Peru to announce your extraordinary discovery. The Peruvian government has decided to leave the treasure in its natural place and make the site a museum. The museum will have a special exhibit showing how you and Sally made the discovery.

When you return home, the round of television appearances and interviews never seems to end; the public can't hear enough about how you and Sally made such a fantastic discovery. After such a brilliant success, you can't wait to turn your attention to other parts of the world, other lost civilizations and treasures.

The End

"They seem very happy here," you observe.

"Yes," Sally agrees. "If we told the world about them, they'd be destroyed. Gold hunters would come, then archaeologists, and finally tourists and souvenir stands."

Eventually it's time for you and Sally to leave. You assure Kalotaxidi and the Inca elders that their secret is safe with you. A part of you is disappointed that you cannot bring news of these pure Inca people to the outside world.

Kalotaxidi promises to take you to a river that will bring you back to the outside world. You wave good-bye to your new Inca friends.

As you set off down the trail, two figures loom, holding rifles. They're filthy, their clothes torn, they look crazed from spending too much time in the jungle. It's Leduc and Maloder!

Leduc stares at you. "Congratulations," he says. "You were quite the toughest to catch. But no quarry ever escapes Paul Leduc. And look where you have led us!"

Leduc pushes you, Sally, and Kalotaxidi ahead of him into the village. Everyone has vanished.

Leduc makes his way to the temple. When he sees the treasure, he goes wild with ecstasy, caresses the gold objects, hugs them. "This is a greater discovery than any Lost City of Gold! I should spare your lives, you have been my good fortune, but credit for this discovery can never be shared!"

Turn to the next page.

Just as Leduc aims his gun, a net made of vines falls from the temple ceiling, knocking him and Maloder to the floor. Incas rush from the dark corners and overpower the two men.

That evening Leduc and Maloder sit tied up in the middle of the temple, surrounded by golden objects. The kiln is fired to its highest temperature. You realize with horror what's going to happen. You've read about an Inca revolt in Cuzco in 1786 and what the rebels did to the Spanish governor.

Two Incas bring a crucible of white-hot molten gold toward the prisoners. The Incas shout at them. You know just what they're saying: "You want gold? You are thirsty for gold? You would die for gold?" Maloder opens his mouth to scream, and they pour the molten gold down his throat. Leduc is white with terror, knowing he will be next.

You and Sally run from the room. No matter what these men deserved, this is too horrible to watch.

The disappearance of the billionaire and a professor on a hunting expedition in the jungle will remain a great mystery.

The End

"Humans," Leduc answers before you can ask. "The Andean Indians of the jungle. Unfortunately the tribe that made the very best quarry is now extinct. We have been discussing how a person from our own culture might be the ultimate test. Especially one who is young, fit, clever."

You gasp as all eyes are fixed on you. "What about a real challenge! Like the latest car-theft video game?" you suggest.

Leduc ignores your comment. "My guests and I are bored. As a good host I have the responsibility to keep them entertained."

"I'm not bored at all," you offer.

"You won't be bored, believe me, as you will be the major event of the weekend," he says, smiling.

Your expression shows Leduc you think he's a savage.

"Ah, I will give you a fair chance," Leduc continues. "If you can evade us for twelve hours, you will be free."

"Do I have a choice?" you ask meekly.

"No. This is my adventure. You have no choice."

Turn to page 106.

You open your eyes, screaming. Mariposa tightly clasps your trembling hands. You're back at Machu Picchu.

You tell those crowded around you what happened.

"Did you see the space ship?" Mariposa asks.

"No, but I'm convinced I came from outer space."

"And the language was like English, you understood it?"

You nod in agreement.

"What you experienced was a future life, not a past life. Past, present, and future are all one in the universe, and you had a glimpse of the future, different clothes, speech, machines, but still humans from this planet." She holds you in her strong, wise gaze.

"So that means I won't discover the treasure in this life." You bow your head in disappointment.

"Not if that's the treasure you're looking for."

"But I don't know if I survived that jaguar's attack! If I did, did I make it out with news of the treasure?"

Mariposa shrugs her shoulders and smiles. "I could hypnotize you again."

"No! No, thank you very much." You've learned enough to know your search in this lifetime is futile. Maybe this knowledge has saved your life—had you continued searching, you might have been lost in the jungle. You're more than happy to go back to your computer and search for another ancient ruin.

The End

CREDITS

Illustrator: Suzanne Nugent received her BFA in illustration from Moore College of Art & Design in Philadelphia Pennsylvania. She now resides with her husband Fred in Philadelphia and works as a freelance illustrator. She first discovered her love for *Choose Your Own Adventure®* books when she was only four years old, which inspired her to become an artist.

Cover Artist: Jose Luis Marron lives and works in Madrid. He has studied film at universities in Canada and France. Jose worked for several years in the Spanish film and television industry, before turning to design and illustration full-time. He has illustrated many *Choose Your Own Adventure®* covers.

This book was brought to life by a great group of people:

    Shannon Gilligan, Publisher

    Gordon Troy, General Counsel

    Jason Gellar, Sales Director

    Melissa Bounty, Senior Editor

    Stacey Boyd, Designer

Thanks to everyone involved!

ABOUT THE AUTHOR

James Becket is a screenwriter and movie director living in Southern California. Before filmmaking he had a varied career: ski racer, eternal student, human rights lawyer, development economist, journalist, author, and international civil servant with the United Nations High Commissioner for Refugees. He graduated from Williams College and Harvard Law School and did graduate work in Switzerland and Chile. He's traveled much of the world with a long time interest in Latin America. He has three daughters: a doctor and an architect who read fairly well, and a seven year-old just learning to read.

**For games, activities and other fun stuff,
or to write to James Becket,
visit us online at CYOA.com**

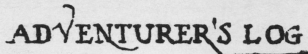

ADVENTURER'S LOG

ADVENTURER'S LOG

Original Fans Love Reading
Choose Your Own Adventure®!

The books let readers remix their own stories—and face the consequences. Kids race to discover lost civilizations, navigate black holes, and go in search of the Yeti, revamped for the 21st century!
Wired Magazine

I love CYOA—I missed CYOA! I've been keeping my fingers as bookmarks on pages 45, 16, 32, and 9 all these years, just to keep my options open.
Madeline, 20

Reading a CYOA book was more like playing a video game on my treasured Nintendo® system. I'm pretty sure the multiple plot twists of *The Lost Jewels of Nabooti* are forever stored in some part of my brain.
The Fort Worth Star Telegram

How I miss you, CYOA! I only have a small shelf left after my mom threw a bunch of you away in a yard sale—she never did understand.
Travis Rex, 26

I LOVE CYOA BOOKS! I have read them since I was a small child. I am so glad to hear they are going back into print! You have just made me the happiest person in the world!
Carey Walker, 27

Inca Gold Trivia Quiz

The Incan ruins have all kinds of mysteries hidden within them. Were you wise enough to locate the Incan gold, or did a more disastrous ending find you instead?

1. What do the Incas describe as "the sweat of the sun"?
A. Lemonade
B. Honey
C. Gold
D. Dog drool

2. You believe you have found an undiscovered Incan settlement
A. With your home computer
B. While on a trek with Sally
C. That aliens have been protecting
D. Next to a shopping mall

3. The settlement you want to travel to is in the dangerous
A. City of Vancouver
B. Soledad Region of Peru
C. Amazonian Rainforest
D. River Nile of Egypt

4. The reclusive billionaire Paul Leduc has a giant black jet with
A. The symbol of the Inca on its nose
B. Twelve televisions on board
C. Swords attached to its wings
D. Mysterious gold-finding powers

5. Machu Pichu was rediscovered by
A. Sally's father
B. A lost dog
C. An American explorer
D. A British monk

6. Maloder attacks you while you are
A. Sleeping in your hotel
B. About to take off on a hang glider
C. At the mouth of a cave of gold
D. Underwater scuba diving

7. When Hernando takes you to the Lost City, you decide to trick him by
A. Impersonating a famous actor
B. Robbing him and leaving him there
C. Leaving a trail of beads to mark the path
D. Pretending you only speak German

8. After Mariposa hypnotizes you, you seem to have traveled
A. Through time
B. To the Bahamas
C. To a world of gold
D. To a different planet

9. Hernando and his twin brother
A. Are both evil
B. Are a mirage
C. Have the same name but different personalities
D. Were separated at birth

10. Your adventure ends in stoning when you come upon a fiesta and
A. Set off fireworks
B. Laugh at the children
C. Eat sacred llama meat
D. Take photographs

THE GOLDEN PATH

ARE YOU READY?

SEVEN BOOK INTERACTIVE EPIC

FOR AGES 12+

INTEGRATED COLLECTABLE CARD GAME